When they all reached her house,
the birds, twittering and singing,
picked up the nest of little ones
and flew back to their home in the park.
Jennie waved good-bye.
"Thank you!" she called.

Jennie's mother helped her wrap the wonderful hat,
piled high with lovely things.
Even after the flowers and leaves had dried,
it would be saved and looked at and remembered
for a long, long time.

Suddenly they all flew away.

On Jennie's head sat the *most* beautiful hat.

At the very top was a nest of chirping young birds!

Jennie felt like chirping too.

Happy from head to toe,

she felt she was walking on air.

People stared in wonder.

Behind her flew the birds,

watchful and proud.

Then
all the birds swooped down together,
flapping and fluttering around Jennie's new hat.

more real flowers,
and a pink valentine.

And two big green and orange leaves,
more pictures,
and some paper flowers,

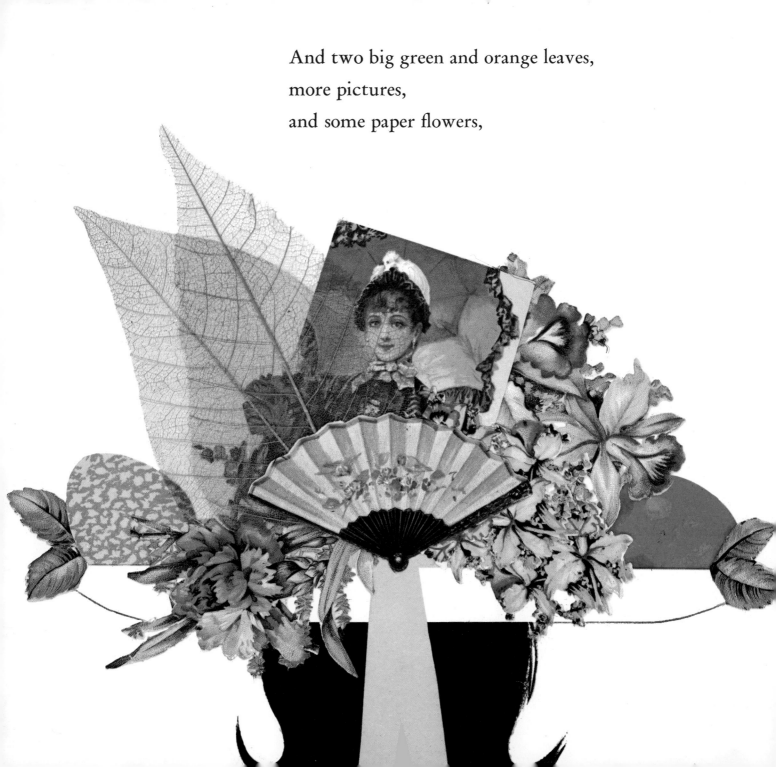

They added
a picture of swans on a quiet lake
and some big red and yellow roses.

They fluttered down to her plain hat,
carrying red and violet flowers,
and leaves,
colored eggs,
and a paper fan.

As they left the church
Jennie saw some birds…
then more and more birds.
Were they following her?

Later, she went to church
with her father, mother, and friends.
All around her hats appeared
like flowers in a garden.

The next morning Jennie got up early
and peeped out the window.
What lovely hats she saw!

But walking home, Jennie remembered, and wished out loud. "Oh, I wish my new hat were just a little fancier."

And birds came!
All sorts of birds,
fluttering
and twittering
and cooing.
They all knew Jennie.
Some ate out of her hand.
Others hopped happily on her head.
Soon every last crumb was gone,
and away they flew!
For a while Jennie forgot about her new hat.

Jennie noticed that it was three o'clock.
Time to feed the birds!
She ran to the cupboard,
filled a paper bag with bread crumbs,
and started for the park.
The birds expected her,
for every Saturday afternoon she went
to the very same spot
to scatter the crumbs.

a TV antenna,

and a shiny pan.
But none of these would do,
not really!

Then she tried on a lampshade,   and a little flower pot,

She put on a straw basket
to see what sort of hat it would make.
Then she drew pictures.
"HAT-CHOO!" she sneezed.
"Bless you, dear," called her mother,
"and what are you doing?"
"I'm drawing a hat-erpillar—
I mean a caterpillar," answered Jennie.
"Oh, dear," sighed her mother. "I see."

She ran to her room and opened the box.

"Oh, no!" she gasped.

"It's such a *plain* hat!"

"Why, dear, I really think it's quite nice,"
her mother said kindly.

Jennie blinked back her tears
and put the hat under her bed.

A new hat!
Jennie's favorite aunt
promised to send her one as a present.
Jennie waited,
and dreamed,
and waited.
Shutting her eyes, she sighed,
"It'll be big,
and flowery,
and oh—
so very beautiful."

At last it came.

JENNIE'S HAT

For Debbie Hautzig

HAT

JEK

JENNIE'S

by EZRA JACK KEATS

Harper & Row, Publishers

1